Harry Potter

THE BATTLE OF HOGWARTS

AND THE MAGIC USED TO DEFEND IT

ISBN 978-1-338-60652-2

10 9 8 7 6 5 4 3 2   22 23 24
Printed in China   95

First edition 2020

Book design by Jessica Meltzer
Written by Cala Spinner and
Daphne Pendergrass

THE BATTLE OF HOGWARTS

"EVERY DAY, EVERY HOUR,
THIS VERY MINUTE PERHAPS,
DARK FORCES ATTEMPT TO PENETRATE
THIS CASTLE'S WALLS.
BUT IN THE END, THEIR
GREATEST WEAPON
IS . . . YOU."

— Albus Dumbledore, *Harry Potter and the Half-Blood Prince*

The Battle of Hogwarts is one of the most iconic moments seen in the Harry Potter films. It tells the story of good versus evil—of Harry versus Voldemort. Said *Harry Potter and the Deathly Hallows – Part 2* director David Yates, "It's the concluding chapter of that universal, age-old battle of what's right and what's good versus what's wrong and what is bad."

In this book, fans will be able to revisit all the exciting cinematic moments from the Battle of Hogwarts and hear from the cast and crew about what it was like to film it.

HARRY POTTER

PORTRAYED BY DANIEL RADCLIFFE

Harry's Wand

"IF ANYONE HERE HAS ANY KNOWLEDGE OF MR. POTTER'S MOVEMENTS THIS EVENING, I INVITE THEM TO STEP FORWARD. NOW."

— Severus Snape,
Harry Potter and the Deathly Hallows – Part 2

In a pivotal movie moment, when Headmaster Severus Snape makes this decree, the Hogwarts students remain quiet. Then, we hear footsteps emerge. It's Harry Potter himself. His appearance marks the beginning of the nearly two-hour-long cinematic Battle of Hogwarts.

THROUGHOUT THE BATTLE OF HOGWARTS ON SCREEN, WE SEE HARRY DO A VARIETY OF BRAVE THINGS, SUCH AS:

- Risk his life to save Draco Malfoy in the burning Room of Requirement.
- Destroy the diadem Horcrux with a Basilisk fang.
- Hurl jinxes at Death Eaters while running through the Hogwarts courtyard.
- Wield the Resurrection Stone.
- Sacrifice himself in the Forbidden Forest to Voldemort.
- Rebound from Voldemort's curse.
- Destroy Voldemort, once and for all.

Basilisk Fang

WHAT'S A BRAVE THING YOU'VE DONE? WHEN DID YOU STAND UP FOR WHAT'S RIGHT? THINK ABOUT IT, THEN USE YOUR WAND PEN TO WRITE THE ANSWER HERE!

_____

_____

_____

_____

_____

DID YOU KNOW?

Voldemort's full name, Tom Marvolo Riddle, with its letters rearranged, spells "I am Lord Voldemort." This is called an anagram.

USING YOUR WAND PEN, WRITE YOUR NAME BELOW, AND THEN WRITE AN ANAGRAM OF YOUR NAME TOO!

_____

_____

LORD VOLDEMORT

PORTRAYED BY CHRISTIAN COULSON, HERO FIENNES-TIFFIN, AND RALPH FIENNES

"ONCE THERE WAS A YOUNG MAN WHO, LIKE YOU, SAT IN THIS VERY HALL, WALKED THIS CASTLE'S CORRIDORS, SLEPT UNDER ITS ROOF. HE SEEMED, TO ALL THE WORLD, A STUDENT LIKE ANY OTHER. HIS NAME? TOM RIDDLE. TODAY, OF COURSE, HE'S KNOWN ALL OVER THE WORLD BY ANOTHER NAME."

— Albus Dumbledore,
Harry Potter and the Half-Blood Prince

Voldemort's influence on Hogwarts can be seen even before the opening credits of the eighth film. Dementors fly high above the castle walls, creating an eerie feel at the otherwise bustling magical school.

When we first see the Voldemort, Harry confides in Ron and Hermione, "It's more like he's wounded . . . He feels more dangerous."

That is how actor Ralph Fiennes chose to portray Voldemort. "I think he'll use anything that helps him come to power, and destroy anything that gets in his way," said Fiennes.

THROUGHOUT THE BATTLE OF HOGWARTS, WE SEE VOLDEMORT:

- Order the execution of Severus Snape.
- Kill Harry in the Forbidden Forest.
- Duel Harry (once he's come back to life) on the Grand Staircase, throughout Hogwarts, and finally, in the school courtyard, where he meets his end.

9

Voldemort's Wand

THE ORDER OF

We first learn about the Order of the Phoenix in the fifth film. "It's an organization dedicated to fighting Voldemort and fighting the Death Eaters," said actor Daniel Radcliffe (Harry Potter). "Dumbledore founded it . . . it means a lot to [Harry] because his parents were in the Order of the Phoenix . . . and I think it's got quite an emotional value to Harry as well as being a chance to fight Voldemort."

In the Battle of Hogwarts, we see the Order burst through the doors of the Great Hall after Harry is revealed, ready for action.

The Order of the Phoenix during the First Wizarding War.

The Order of the Phoenix during the Battle of Hogwarts.

THE PHOENIX

ALBUS DUMBLEDORE
Portrayed by Richard Harris and Michael Gambon

Albus Dumbledore was the Headmaster of Hogwarts School of Witchcraft and Wizardry and the proud face of a Chocolate Frog trading card.

KINGSLEY SHACKLEBOLT
Portrayed by George Harris

Kingsley Shacklebolt was an Auror. His Patronus— a lynx—warned the guests at Bill and Fleur's wedding of the Death Eaters' arrival in *Harry Potter and the Deathly Hallows – Part 1.*

MINERVA MCGONAGALL
Portrayed by Maggie Smith

Minerva McGonagall taught Transfiguration at Hogwarts. In the Battle of Hogwarts, Professor McGonagall dueled Snape and enchanted the castle's statues to help defend it.

NYMPHADORA TONKS
Portrayed by Natalia Tena

Tonks was a Metamorphmagus; she could change her appearance at will. She fought in many battles, but lost her life in the Battle of Hogwarts.

ALASTOR MOODY
Portrayed by Brendan Gleeson

We meet "Mad-Eye" Moody in the fourth film; however, he was a Death Eater in disguise. Later, Mad-Eye lost his life in the Battle of the Seven Potters.

ARABELLA FIGG
Portrayed by Kathryn Hunter

Arabella Figg was not a witch; however, she was born to magical parents, making her a Squib. Arabella served the Order of the Phoenix as a spy.

← WHO WAS THE ORDER OF THE PHOENIX FIGHTING, ASIDE FROM VOLDEMORT? SAY **LUMOS** AND USE YOUR WAND TO REVEAL SECRETS ABOUT THE DEATH EATERS IN THE PAGES THAT FOLD OUT.

AMYCUS AND ALECTO CARROW
Portrayed by Suzie Toase and Ralph Ineson

• Death Eaters
• Siblings
• Hogwarts Professors

"They like punishment, the Carrows."
—Neville Longbottom, *Harry Potter and the Deathly Hallows – Part 2*

Propmakers took inspiration from Mogul arabesque patterns for the Death Eaters' masks. Each one has its own engravings and motifs. Although the masks were used during most Wizarding War battles, they weren't in the Battle of Hogwarts, as the Death Eaters weren't hiding.

USING YOUR WAND PEN, DESIGN A MASK BELOW!

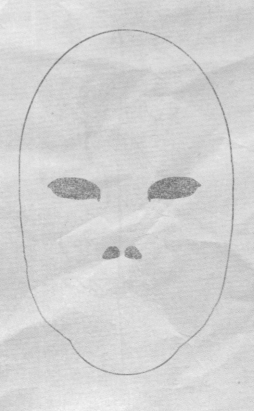

BELLATRIX LESTRANGE
Portrayed by Helena Bonham Carter

- Voldemort's right-hand witch
- Devout Death Eater
- Murdered Sirius Black
- Defeated by Molly Weasley

"I think she genuinely loves Voldemort. And she's a genuine follower of Voldemort." —Helena Bonham Carter (Bellatrix Lestrange)

ANTONIN DOLOHOV
Portrayed by Arben Bajraktaraj

- Attempted to capture Harry inside a Muggle café
- Mind wiped by Hermione
- Defeated in the Battle of Hogwarts

"This is Dolohov. I recognize him from the wanted posters." —Ron Weasley, *Harry Potter and the Deathly Hallows – Part 1*

PETER PETTIGREW
Portrayed by Timothy Spall

- Animagus: Rat
- Betrayed Lily and James Potter
- Double Agent
- Helped resurrect the Dark Lord

"[Peter] is by nature a cringer and someone who would always beg for pity. But underneath it, he's always conniving, he's always planning. As soon as the other person is not looking, he takes his advantage." —Timothy Spall (Peter Pettigrew)

ALBUS PERCIVAL WULFERIC BRIAN DUMBLEDORE

PORTRAYED BY RICHARD HARRIS AND MICHAEL GAMBON

"HARRY, YOU'RE SAFE. AS LONG AS DUMBLEDORE'S AROUND, YOU CAN'T BE TOUCHED."

— Hermione Granger, *Harry Potter and the Sorcerer's Stone*

In the Battle of Hogwarts, we see a spirit version of Dumbledore provide counsel to Harry in King's Cross station in Harry's mind. "I'm only back for two weeks," actor Michael Gambon (Albus Dumbledore) said, while filming *Harry Potter and the Deathly Hallows – Part 2*. "Just as a ghost." But, as the wise Dumbledore tells Harry in the film, "Why should that mean that it's not real?"

Dumbledore's Wand

DID YOU KNOW?

Actor Michael Gambon took over the role from Richard Harris in the third film. Although he adopted a new approach for Dumbledore, he kept a slight Irish accent reminiscent of Harris's.

RONALD WEASLEY

PORTRAYED BY RUPERT GRINT

Ron's Wand

"WELL, RON WAS THINKING— IT WAS RON'S IDEA, IT'S COMPLETELY BRILLIANT."

—Hermione Granger, *Harry Potter and the Deathly Hallows – Part 2*

During the Battle of Hogwarts, Ron imitated Harry speaking Parseltongue to enter the Chamber of Secrets and retrieve a Basilisk fang.

The last time Harry Potter fans saw the Chamber of Secrets was nine years prior, in *Harry Potter and the Chamber of Secrets*. Actor Rupert Grint (Ron Weasley) recalled, "It was really weird seeing that set again. It's one of the best sets. The skeleton of the Basilisk was where we left it, but it was eerie going back there."

HERMIONE GRANGER

PORTRAYED BY EMMA WATSON

Hermione's Wand

"ONE OF MY BEST FRIENDS IS MUGGLE-BORN. SHE'S THE BEST IN OUR YEAR."

—Harry Potter, *Harry Potter and the Half-Blood Prince*

Hermione Granger has plenty of hero moments in the Battle of Hogwarts.

Actress Emma Watson (Hermione Granger) said, "I've never run down, or run up and down so many stairs in my entire life. But it's very brave. She definitely plays her part well."

We also see Hermione delve deep into the Chamber of Secrets, sling curses at Death Eaters, and offer to sacrifice herself alongside Harry so that he wouldn't go to Voldemort alone. Hermione proves herself to be brave in the face of adversity.

DUMBLEDORE'S ARMY

In *Harry Potter and the Order of the Phoenix*, Harry formed Dumbledore's Army—a secret student organization that met to learn Defense Against the Dark Arts. Dumbledore's Army, also known as the DA, fought alongside the Order of the Phoenix in many battles. Some former DA members—like Fred and George Weasley—even became fully-fledged Order of the Phoenix members upon leaving Hogwarts. This group proved instrumental to the demise of Voldemort. As we see in the fifth film, Hermione asked all DA members to sign a slip of paper. Turn the page to reveal some of the members of Dumbledore's Army.

NEVILLE LONGBOTTOM

HOUSE: Gryffindor
PORTRAYED BY: Matthew Lewis

Neville Longbottom exhibited an immense amount of courage in the Battle of Hogwarts. Lewis said, "Suddenly by the last film, he is this reckless freedom fighter who doesn't care about his own safety. He just wants to do the right thing." We witness Neville deliver an impassioned speech about not giving up. He goes on to defeat Nagini.

GINNY WEASLEY

HOUSE: Gryffindor
PORTRAYED BY: Bonnie Wright

In the Battle of Hogwarts, Ginny can be seen dodging Death Eaters' attacks, and notably attempts to fight Voldemort when he announces that Harry is dead. Wright recalled, "It was really epic and spectacular. Then Voldemort has this speech, and Ginny screams at him—the one person who is the most feared wizard in the whole world. It was quite daunting."

DEAN THOMAS

HOUSE: Gryffindor
PORTRAYED BY: Alfred Enoch

Talking about the Battle of Hogwarts, Enoch said, "You're faced with two hundred Death Eaters who are coming at you. And they, I tell you, were a terrifying sight. It was decided that Dean and Seamus would do their best to stand their ground. With Ralph Fiennes (Voldemort) coming towards you looking demonic and very terrifying, it wasn't an easy thing to do."

FRED AND GEORGE WEASLEY

HOUSE: Gryffindor
PORTRAYED BY: Oliver and James Phelps

Fred and George left Hogwarts under Umbridge's regime and founded a joke shop. "They kind of make the best out of everything," said Oliver. After leaving the DA, they became members of the Order of the Phoenix alongside their family. George suffered an ear injury in the Battle of the Seven Potters. Fred met a fatal end in the Battle of Hogwarts.

LUNA LOVEGOOD

HOUSE: Ravenclaw
PORTRAYED BY: Evanna Lynch

In the Battle of Hogwarts, Luna helped Harry locate Rowena Ravenclaw's diadem. With director David Yates's help, Lynch realized that it was Luna's moment to save the world. "So then she just screams at Harry and says, 'Harry Potter, you listen to me right now!'"

SEAMUS FINNIGAN

HOUSE: Gryffindor
PORTRAYED BY: Devon Murray

Seamus was a half-blood wizard with an affinity for lighting things on fire. During the Battle of Hogwarts, Professor McGonagall told Seamus to blow up the Wooden Bridge. This act prevented Death Eaters from accessing to the castle. Murray said the Battle of Hogwarts was, "the worst battle we've had, but it was great to have a bit of fun and defend Hogwarts and everyone else."

LAVENDER BROWN

HOUSE: Gryffindor
PORTRAYED BY: Jessie Cave, Kathleen Cauley, and Jennifer Smith

Lavender was a witch who fought in the Battle of Hogwarts, but can be seen tragically bitten by a werewolf. Hermione blasted the werewolf away, though Lavender's fate is unclear. Cave said, "It was so scary for everyone because the safe place of Hogwarts had been intruded."

USE YOUR PEN TO ADD YOUR NAME TO THE LIST OF STUDENTS
WHO WERE MEMBERS OF DUMBLEDORE'S ARMY.

Dumbledore's Army

Padma Patil

Katie Bell

Zacharias Smith

Parvati Patil

Cho Chang

THE WEASLEY FAMILY

Almost all the Weasleys were members of either the Order of the Phoenix or Dumbledore's Army.

During the Battle of Hogwarts, Molly Weasley, matriarch of the family, defeated Bellatrix Lestrange when she attempted to harm Ginny. "It's great that it's in there, and that it's Molly Weasley, who's the most unexpected person to do it," actress Julie Walters (Molly Weasley) said of the moment.

Bill and Fleur helped Harry, Ron, and Hermione hide at Shell Cottage in *Harry Potter and the Deathly Hallows – Parts 1* and *2*, and Charlie can be spotted at Bill and Fleur's wedding, helping the guests reach safety. Arthur, meanwhile, can be seen back-to-back with Kingsley Shacklebolt in a scene in *Harry Potter and the Deathly Hallows – Part 2*, sending one of Voldemort's followers through a window.

Gryffindor Banner

GRYFFINDOR

THE MALFOY FAMILY

Draco Malfoy and Harry established a rivalry in the first film that continued through the series. Draco's father, Lucius, was a Death Eater. His mother, Narcissa, was never an official Death Eater herself, but her sister Bellatrix Lestrange was.

In the sixth film, Draco is drafted to work undercover for Voldemort. However, in *Harry Potter and the Deathly Hallows – Part 2*, things change. "I think the Malfoys have got rather an interesting journey in the second film," said Jason Isaacs (Lucius Malfoy). "There's a lot of moral conflict."

During the Battle of Hogwarts, Narcissa checked Harry to see if the Dark Lord had killed him. She lied and said that he did. This gave Narcissa enough time to sneak away with Lucius and Draco, unharmed, and allowed Harry to attack Voldemort with the element of surprise. Here, Narcissa demonstrated the most powerful magic of all: love.

Lucius Malfoy's Wand

SEVERUS SNAPE

PORTRAYED BY ALAN RICKMAN, ALEC HOPKINS, AND BENEDICT CLARKE

"ALBUS SEVERUS POTTER. YOU WERE NAMED AFTER TWO HEADMASTERS OF HOGWARTS. ONE OF THEM WAS A SLYTHERIN, AND HE WAS THE BRAVEST MAN I'VE EVER KNOWN."

—Harry Potter, *Harry Potter and the Deathly Hallows – Part 2*

We learn in the interlude of the Battle of Hogwarts that although Severus Snape was a Death Eater in the First Wizarding War, he changed allegiance to the Order of the Phoenix—and to Dumbledore—after Voldemort killed Lily Potter, Harry's mother. Snape was in love with Lily since their childhood and remained in love with her until her death.

Snape was a double agent. He was a master at Potions, Occlumency, and Legilimency. In the Battle of Hogwarts, Voldemort ordered his snake, Nagini, to kill Snape in order to gain possession of the Elder Wand.

David Yates, the director on the last four films, said, "What Alan does with Snape—you hang on every breath and every pause. And there isn't an actor who I've worked with who's delivered lines as slowly as Alan, but he delivers them in a way that makes you wait and wait and wait, because you want to hear what's coming next."

Snape's Wand

Severus and Lily in their youth.

Sirius's Wand

> "I TAUGHT THE WHOLE **BLACK FAMILY** EXCEPT SIRIUS. IT'S A SHAME. TALENTED BOY."
>
> — Horace Slughorn,
> *Harry Potter and the Half-Blood Prince*

P rior to the Battle of Hogwarts, Sirius Black was an integral member of the Order of the Phoenix. He provided his ancestral house, 12 Grimmauld Place, as its headquarters. He was also Harry's godfather. Some words of wisdom he gave Harry were, "We've all got both light and dark inside of us, what matters is the part we choose to act on."

Actor Gary Oldman (Sirius Black) admitted that quote was special to him. "I showed that to my son. I said, 'Read that line,'" Oldman recalled.

Unfortunately, Sirius was murdered by his cousin Bellatrix Lestrange in the Battle of the Department of Mysteries. A version of him appears to Harry during the Battle of Hogwarts and offers encouragement when Harry uses the Resurrection Stone.

WHAT'S THE BEST ADVICE YOU'VE EVER GOTTEN?
THINK ABOUT IT, THEN WRITE IT BELOW!

_____

_____

_____

_____

_____

REMUS LUPIN

PORTRAYED BY DAVID THEWLIS AND JAMES UTECHIN

"HE'S A WEREWOLF."

— Hermione Granger, *Harry Potter and the Prisoner of Azkaban*

We first meet Remus Lupin in *Harry Potter and the Prisoner of Azkaban*. As Defense Against the Dark Arts professor, Lupin taught his third years valuable lessons, including how to defend themselves against Boggarts. He also taught Harry the Patronus Charm.

"He's one of the last surviving links Harry has to his parents," actor David Thewlis (Remus Lupin) said about the character. "And he's a great comfort to Harry."

After leaving Hogwarts, Lupin joined the Order of the Phoenix. During the Second Wizarding War, he met Tonks, whom he married and had a son, Teddy. However, Teddy was left orphaned—not unlike Harry in the First Wizarding War—after the monumental battle.

PETER PETTIGREW

PORTRAYED BY TIMOTHY SPALL AND CHARLES HUGHES

> "TONIGHT, HE WHO BETRAYED HIS FRIENDS, WHOSE HEART ROTS WITH MURDER, SHALL BREAK FREE. INNOCENT BLOOD SHALL BE SPILT . . . AND SERVANT AND MASTER SHALL BE REUNITED ONCE MORE."
>
> — Professor Trelawney, *Harry Potter and the Prisoner of Azkaban*

We first meet Peter Pettigrew in *Harry Potter and the Sorcerer's Stone,* but we don't know it yet. After framing Sirius for the murder of Lily and James Potter, Peter faked his death and hid in his rat Animagus form. Coincidentally, he became Ron's animal companion.

This secret is discovered in the third film. Peter escaped and returned to the Dark Lord. Actor Timothy Spall (Peter Pettigrew) had to construct the human version of Scabbers and bring him to the screen.

"I just felt that because of the whole look, the suit and the hair, when I have the teeth in . . . I just started to feel that the character's natural stance would be kind of rat-like, you know, kind of ready to jump, or ready to be subservient," Spall said.

SECOND WIZARDING WAR FIGHTS

INFILTRATION OF THE MINISTRY OF MAGIC

In *Deathly Hallows – Part 1*, Voldemort took over the Ministry of Magic. Muggle-borns were rounded up and put on trial, accused of stealing their wands. Amid all this, Harry, Hermione, and Ron were in hiding, seeking Voldemort's Horcruxes. They needed to impersonate Ministry officials in order to retrieve the locket Horcrux that was located there. When their disguises wore off, a battle ensued.

GODRIC'S HOLLOW

In *Deathly Hallows – Part 1*, Harry and Hermione discovered Bathilda Bagshot in Godric's Hollow. However, the woman was actually Voldemort's snake, Nagini, in disguise. Harry's wand was broken in the turmoil, which led to him borrowing Hermione's.

SKIRMISH AT MALFOY MANOR

Also in *Deathly Hallows – Part 1*, Harry, Ron, and Hermione were captured by the Snatchers and taken to Malfoy Manor. Rupert Grint (Ron Weasley) noted, "It's a tense time. Hermione gives Harry this stinging jinx that makes him unrecognizable. If they find out it's Harry, it's all over and Voldemort wins." Dobby the house-elf evidently freed the trio—along with Luna Lovegood and Garrick Ollivander, the wandmaker—but the fight was dangerous. Dobby ended up losing his life to the cause.

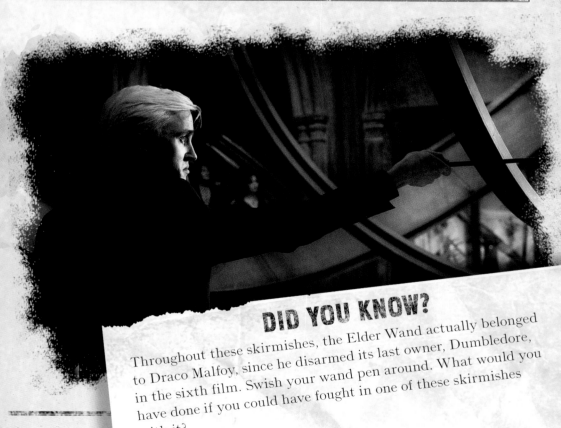

DID YOU KNOW?

Throughout these skirmishes, the Elder Wand actually belonged to Draco Malfoy, since he disarmed its last owner, Dumbledore, in the sixth film. Swish your wand pen around. What would you have done if you could have fought in one of these skirmishes with it?

BATTLES OF THE
SECOND WIZARDING WAR

We see the Second Wizarding War play out over the course of three years, from the end of Harry's fourth year to what would have been the end of his seventh. Over that time, there was a multitude of battles, skirmishes, and attacks by Death Eaters on the Order of the Phoenix and other innocents.

SAY **REVELIO!** AND USE YOUR WAND TO REVEAL MORE ABOUT THIS KEY SCENE FROM THE FILMS. ➡

THE BATTLE OF THE DEPARTMENT OF MYSTERIES

A s seen in the fifth film, the Battle of the Department of Mysteries pitted Dumbledore's Army and the Order of the Phoenix against Voldemort.

"This is the time that we get to see some Olympic-level ninja wandage," said Jason Isaacs (Lucius Malfoy). He added that, among the cast and choreographers, they developed a vocabulary. "We've got a physical vocabulary for wands, which isn't fencing and isn't pointe and isn't dancing, but it's—it's something."

The cast and crew spent tons of time choreographing the battle just right.

PETRIFICUS TOTALUS
Pronunciation:
pe-TRI-fi-kus to-TAH-lus

The Body-Bind Curse stiffens the target's limbs so they cannot move. Neville learned the spell during DA meetings and used it in the Department of Mysteries.

PROTEGO
Pronunciation: proh-TAY-goh

The Shield Charm *Protego* is used to create a protective shield around the caster. We see Harry use this in the Department of Mysteries to block Lucius Malfoy's curse.

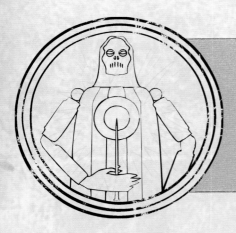

REDUCTO
Pronunciation: reh-DUCK-toe

Reducto is used to blast solid objects to pieces. Ginny Weasley learned this spell at DA meetings. She used it against a Death Eater in the Battle of the Department of Mysteries.

STUPEFY
Pronunciation: STOO-puh-fy

Stupefy causes an opponent to fly backward and renders them unconscious. It's seen many times throughout the Battle of the Department of Mysteries, cast by Hermione, Harry, Neville, and Lucius Malfoy.

SPELLS USED IN THE
DEPARTMENT OF MYSTERIES

Choreographers worked with the cast and crew to make sure each spell had a unique movement. In the films, we see a variety of fantastic and beautiful magic in this scene. Discover the spells that were used by lighting your wand below!

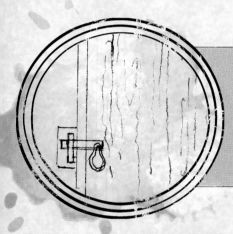

ALOHOMORA
Pronunciation: ah-LOH-ho-MOR-ah

Alohomora, the Unlocking Charm, is used to unlock a locked object, such as a door. In the fifth film, Harry used this spell to no avail in trying to unlock the Room of Doors.

FIENDFYRE

This Dark curse conjures flames that take the form of creatures (such as serpents) that hunt down the caster's target. Lord Voldemort used it on Dumbledore but Dumbledore defeats it.

LEVICORPUS
Pronunciation: leh-vee-COR-pus

This jinx lifts the target into the air by the ankle and leaves them dangling upside-down. Luna Lovegood can be seen using it against Death Eaters in the Battle of the Department of Mysteries.

THE BATTLE OF THE SEVEN POTTERS

I n *Deathly Hallows – Part 1*, Harry fled the Dursleys' house to safety. To do so, the Order of the Phoenix arranged for six volunteers to impersonate Harry, along with a magical protector, to safeguard his identity. Of course, this meant that actor Daniel Radcliffe (Harry Potter) had to shoot this scene seven times!

"We'd shoot one version with me as one of the characters, and then the camera would stay in exactly the same place and we'd shoot another version with me as another character, and then they'd just lay them on top of each other," Radcliffe said. "We did get up to, I think, ninety-five takes on that one. It was a long day."

KEY PLAYERS

HARRY POTTER

FRED WEASLEY

GEORGE WEASLEY

MUNDUNGUS FLETCHER

FLEUR DELACOUR

RON WEASLEY

HERMIONE GRANGER

THE SEVEN PROTECTORS: Mad-Eye Moody, Bill Weasley, Arthur Weasley, Remus Lupin, Nymphadora Tonks, Kingsley Shacklebolt, Rubeus Hagrid

IF YOU COULD USE POLYJUICE POTION TO TURN INTO ANYONE, WHO WOULD IT BE AND WHY? USE YOUR WAND PEN TO WRITE YOUR ANSWER HERE!

_____

_____

_____

_____

_____

_____

VOLDEMORT'S

As we see Professor Slughorn tell Tom Riddle in a memory in *Harry Potter and the Half-Blood Prince*, Horcruxes are Dark magical objects. They contain a bit of a person's soul and are created by killing. So long as the person's soul is encapsulated in an object, they cannot fully die.

Jim Broadbent (Slughorn) admits that giving Tom this information was a mistake Slughorn carried with him for decades. "He bears it very heavily, really, this secret and he's reluctant to talk about it." Voldemort managed to create seven Horcuxes—six intentional, one not.

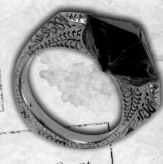

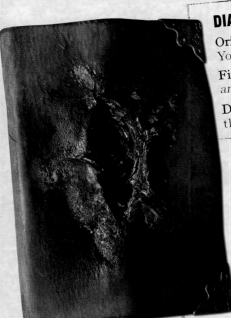

DIARY
Originally Owned By: Young Tom Marvolo Riddle

First Seen In: *Harry Potter and the Chamber of Secrets*

Destroyed By: Harry, with the Basilisk fang

RING
Originally Owned By: Marvolo Gaunt (Voldemort's maternal grandfather)

First Seen In: *Harry Potter and the Half-Blood Prince*

Destroyed By: Professor Dumbledore, with the Sword of Gryffindor

LOCKET
Originally Owned By: Salazar Slytherin

First Seen In: *Harry Potter and the Half-Blood Prince* (as a fake)

Destroyed By: Ron Weasley, with the Sword of Gryffindor

HORCRUXES

NAGINI

First Seen In: *Harry Potter and the Goblet of Fire*

Destroyed By: Neville Longbottom, with the Sword of Gryffindor

CUP

Originally Owned By: Helga Hufflepuff

First Seen In: *Harry Potter and the Deathly Hallows – Part 1*

Destroyed By: Hermione Granger, with the Basilisk fang in the Chamber of Secrets

DIADEM

Originally Owned By: Rowena Ravenclaw

First Seen In: *Harry Potter and the Deathly Hallows – Part 2*

Destroyed By: Harry Potter, Ron Weasley, and Gregory Goyle, who inadvertently created the Fiendfyre that Ron kicks it into

HARRY POTTER

Harry was the last Horcrux that Voldemort didn't intend to create. He sacrificed himself to Voldemort's Killing Curse but then chose to go back and finish the fight.

Destroyed By: Voldemort, with the Killing Curse

DID YOU KNOW?

Before the seventh book was published, actor Daniel Radcliffe (Harry Potter) asked J.K. Rowling if Harry died. Rowling replied, "You get a death scene."

THE BATTLE

E very character, duel, and moment in the Harry Potter films leads up to the Battle of Hogwarts.

"This is the final battle for Hogwarts, and the final battle for the wizarding world, and something we've been building to throughout this series," said producer David Heyman.

The Battle of Hogwarts took place in several sets. Propmakers and set designers used elements of other films within this film, such as placing the wizard's chess pieces from *Harry Potter and the Sorcerer's Stone* in the Room of Requirement, as well as the animal skeleton hanging in Gilderoy Lockhart's classroom.

THE HOG'S HEAD INN

The Hog's Head Inn is located in Hogsmeade. It's owned by Professor Dumbledore's brother, Aberforth. Harry, Ron, Hermione, and Neville use it to enter Hogwarts castle in secret.

THE GREAT HALL

This set is used many times, including McGonagall's wand duel with Snape. Actress Dame Maggie Smith (Minerva McGonagall) originally thought the fight would be more physical. "But wands work in a magical way. I don't know how the fight will turn out or what magic will come out of the ends of it," she admitted, since the wand special effects are added in post-production.

OF HOGWARTS

THE GRAND STAIRCASE

The Grand Staircase is all but destroyed in the Battle of Hogwarts. "It's kind of sad to see all these kind of sets we've grown up with . . . just destroyed, really. All the rubble everywhere, and I'm on the moving staircase with all these portraits all being kind of ripped . . . It's quite shocking, really," said Rupert Grint (Ron Weasley).

THE ROOM OF REQUIREMENT

The Room of Requirement was destroyed when Gregory Goyle used Fiendfyre against Ron, Hermione, and Harry. According to set dresser Stephenie McMillan, when she and the film's production designer were designing the set and creating the piles and piles of furniture in the room, they used dollhouse furniture to model it. McMillan recalls, "And for every tiny chair that was bought, we had to buy real chairs. I think we must have had at least two thousand chairs in there."

WOODEN BRIDGE

The Wooden Bridge is destroyed in the Battle of Hogwarts by Seamus Finnigan, who blew it up in order to keep the Death Eaters out of Hogwarts.

Did you know? The Wooden Bridge set was added to Hogwarts by director Alfonso Cuarón in *Harry Potter and the Prisoner of Azkaban*.

THE CHAMBER OF SECRETS

Ron imitated the Parseltongue that Harry spoke in his sleep to open the entrance to the Chamber of Secrets, and Hermione destroyed the diadem Horcrux. This is also where we see Ron and Hermione's first kiss. "And I think in the moment, it's about both of them realizing . . . if we're going to die tonight, the one thing I actually want to do is kiss you. And so it's quite romantic," recalled Emma Watson (Hermione Granger).

THE FORBIDDEN FOREST

In the eighth film, Harry sacrifices himself to Voldemort in the Forbidden Forest. "When Harry comes to face [Voldemort] alone in the forest, I think he feels, you know, more confident—as the boy who lived come to die," said producer David Heyman. However, Harry chose to return after Voldemort destroyed the Horcrux within him.

THE CLOCK TOWER

Just before their final duel, which takes place in multiple locales around the castle, Harry and Voldemort crashed into the Clock Tower. "It's very physical," Ralph Fiennes (Voldemort) said of the scene. "We started doing it when Harry grabs me and pulls me off the battlements, pulls me by the neck, and we're turning and turning in a sort of twisting entanglement of spirits and bodies fighting and wrestling and falling to the ground."

SPELLS

A multitude of spells, jinxes, hexes, and magic can be seen in the Battle of Hogwarts.

PIERTOTUM LOCOMOTOR

PRONUNCIATION: pee-eer-TOE-tuhm low-kuh-MOH-tor

"I'VE ALWAYS WANTED TO USE THAT SPELL."

— Minerva McGonagall, *Harry Potter and the Deathly Hallows – Part 2*

This spell makes a previously inanimate object come to life. Professor McGonagall cast it during the Battle of Hogwarts, bringing all the knight statues of the castle to defend against attackers.

PATRONUSES CAN TAKE MANY FORMS. WHAT WOULD YOURS LOOK LIKE? FIND THE SIX PATRONUSES HIDING ON THIS PAGE. THEN DRAW YOUR OWN IN INVISIBLE INK!

Harry Potter: Stag

Hermione Granger: Otter

Ron Weasley: Jack Russell Terrier

Luna Lovegood: Hare

Cho Chang: Swan

Ginny Weasley: Horse

Draw your
Patronus here!

EXPECTO PATRONUM

PRONUNCIATION: eck-SPEK-toe pah-TROH-nuhm

Expecto Patronum, the Patronus Charm, is used to conjure a magical guardian in the form of an animal to protect its caster. It is the only known defense against Dementors. A caster must draw from their happiest and most powerful memory to produce it.

After learning the charm in the third film, Harry passed his knowledge along to Dumbledore's Army in *Harry Potter and the Order of the Phoenix*, teaching all the members how to conjure full-bodied, corporeal Patronuses.

Actress Evanna Lynch (Luna Lovegood) found filming this spell difficult, as she had to imagine her spirit guardian in the room, which was added in later by the special effects team.

MOLLY WEASLEY'S CURSE

In the Battle of Hogwarts, when her daughter Ginny fell across the path of Bellatrix Lestrange, Molly stunned and destroyed the witch. When discussing Molly Weasley's turn as an action hero, actress Julie Walters noted, "I love the fact that a woman defeats her. And it's Mrs. Weasley, who is the symbol of maternal good."

REPELLO
(MUGGLETUM OR INIMICUM)

PRONUNCIATION:
reh-PELL-oh
(MUH-guhl-tuhm or ihn-ih-MIH-kum)

Repello repels people from a certain area. Professor Flitwick can be seen using a version of this spell prior to the Death Eaters' arrival at the Battle of Hogwarts in order to protect the castle.

CONFRINGO

PRONUNCIATION:
con-FRING-oh

Confringo, the Blasting Curse, causes the target to explode in a fiery blast. In the Battle of Hogwarts, Harry uses this curse after coming back from the "dead."

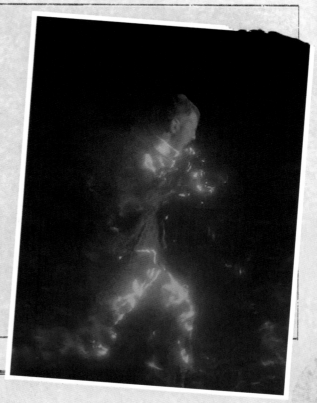

SONORUS

PRONUNCIATION: sohn-OAR-us

The Amplifying Charm, *Sonorus*, makes its target much louder than before. In the Battle of Hogwarts, Lord Voldemort used a version of this charm to communicate with the students. Actor Ralph Fiennes admitted that he used a special voice to portray the Dark Lord. "It's sort of a hoarse, whispery quality. There's something serpentine about it," he said.

DESCENDO

PRONUNCIATION: deh-SEN-doh

Descendo is cast to make an object fall. In the Battle of Hogwarts, we see Harry cast this spell several times in the burning Room of Requirement to cause piles of junk to fall in the path of the out-of-control Fiendfyre.

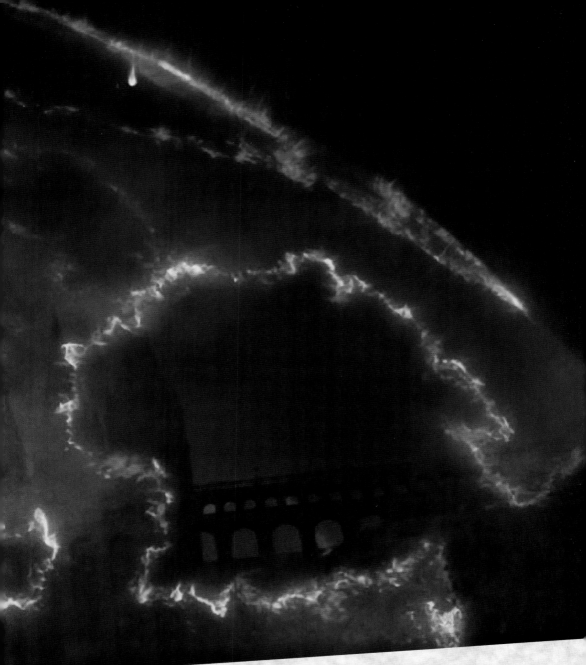

PROTEGO MAXIMA

PRONUNCIATION: proh-TAY-goh MAK-see-mah

Multiple casters use this variation of *Protego* to create a strong shield around the castle during the Battle of Hogwarts. The spell was combined with *Fianto Duri* (which makes the shield more resistant to attacks) and *Repello Inimicum* (which repels enemies). Casters included Professor Filius Flitwick, Professor Horace Slughorn, and Molly Weasley.

CAPACIOUS EXTRMIS

PRONUNCIATION: ca-PAY-shus ex-TREHM-us

Capacious Extremis, otherwise known as the Undetectable Extension Charm, is a charm that allows the caster to extend the space inside an object, without making the object any heavier.

Hermione used this spell to enchant her small beaded handbag, which is then used to carry enough supplies to last her, Ron, and Harry a full year on the run in *Harry Potter and the Deathly Hallows – Part 1*. "It's definitely a very useful invention of hers," Emma Watson (Hermione Granger) said. "She's so clever."

SOME ITEMS KEPT IN HERMIONE'S BAG

The Monster
Book of Monsters

Essence of
Dittany

The Sword of
Gryffindor

THINK ABOUT WHAT YOU'D PUT IN A BAG LIKE HERMIONE'S. THEN WRITE FIVE IDEAS HERE!

1. _____

2. _____

3. _____

4. _____

5. _____

DIFFINDO

PRONUNCIATION: dih-FINN-doe

Diffindo, more commonly known as the Severing Charm, is used to cut through an object. Harry employed this charm in *Harry Potter and the Deathly Hallows – Part 1* to split the ice on a frozen pond to retrieve the Sword of Gryffindor.

DISSENDIUM

PRONUNCIATION: dih-SEN-dee-uhm

Dissendium is a spell that reveals secret passages. Harry learned about this spell in his third year from the Marauder's Map. Harry tried to use this spell to destroy or reveal more information from the locket Horcrux but it did not work.

Neville practicing *Expelliarmus* in a Dumbledore's Army meeting.

EXPELLIARMUS

PRONUNCIATION: eck-SPELL-ee-AR-muss

"DON'T EVEN THINK ABOUT IT."

—Harry Potter to Gilderoy Lockhart, *Harry Potter and the Chamber of Secrets*

Expelliarmus, the Disarming Charm, is one of the most popular spells used throughout the films. Its main purpose is to cause the target to drop whatever they are holding, usually their wand. Harry famously defeated Lord Voldemort with this spell.

"And, as I again throw the Elder Wand Killing Spell at Harry, he matches it with his power. The power spells hover, and finally mine rebounds back at me again. And because I'm fully weakened now . . . [Voldemort] dies," Ralph Fiennes (Voldemort) explained.

PRIORI INCANTATEM

PRONUNCIATION: pri-OR-ee in-can-TAH-tem

This spell forces a wand to repeat (or remember) its last motions.

NOTABLE CAST

In the graveyard following the Triwizard Tournament, Voldemort's wand reveals the spirits of those he'd most recently murdered, including Cedric Diggory and Harry's parents.

PRIORI INCANTATEM IS A VERY RARE, VERY POWERFUL SPELL THAT'S ALL ABOUT MEMORY. CAN YOU REMEMBER THE LAST FIVE BOOKS YOU'VE READ? WRITE THEM DOWN HERE!

1. _____

2. _____

3. _____

4. _____

5. _____

UNFORGIVABLE CURSES

The three Unforgivable Curses are known as the Imperius Curse, the Cruciatus Curse, and the Killing Curse. They are called "unforgivable" because using any of them is forbidden. However, all were commonly employed in the Battle of Hogwarts.

Barty Crouch Jr., posing as Defense Against the Dark Arts professor Alastor Moody, taught his students these curses in the fourth film.

"He wants them to face the fact that evil exists and that they better face up to it," said Brendan Gleeson (Mad-Eye Moody). "They're going to be embroiled in these things soon enough and they better know what they're getting themselves into."

IMPERIO

PRONUNCIATION: im-PEER-ee-oh

The Imperius Curse (*Imperio*) places the target completely under the caster's control.

We see Barty Crouch Jr., disguised as Mad-Eye Moody, perform this on a spider in front of his fourth-year students.

In the eighth film, Harry used this curse on a goblin at Gringotts Wizarding Bank in order to gain access to Bellatrix Lestrange's vault and the cup Horcrux inside.

Ron used this on the goblin again at Gringotts after passing through Thief's Downfall.

CRUCIO

PRONUNCIATION: KROO-see-oh

"FOURTEEN YEARS AGO, A DEATH EATER NAMED BELLATRIX LESTRANGE USED A CRUCIATUS CURSE ON MY PARENTS. SHE TORTURED THEM FOR INFORMATION, BUT THEY NEVER GAVE IN."

—Neville Longbottom, *Harry Potter and the Order of the Phoenix*

The Cruciatus Curse (*Crucio*) causes a target immense physical pain.

Bellatrix Lestrange used the curse to torture Neville Longbottom's Auror parents to the point of insanity during the First Wizarding War.

Voldemort used this curse on Harry twice during their duel in the Little Hangleton graveyard.

In the fifth film, Professor Umbridge threatens to use this curse on Harry after he breaks into her office.

After she killed Sirius Black, Harry used this curse on Bellatrix. This is his first time using an Unforgivable Curse.

Bellatrix showed her preference for the curse once more after Harry, Ron, and Hermione are imprisoned at Malfoy Manor, where she tortured Hermione for information.

AVADA KEDAVRA

"THE KILLING CURSE. ONLY ONE PERSON'S KNOWN TO HAVE SURVIVED IT, AND HE'S SITTING IN THIS ROOM."

—Barty Crouch Jr. (disguised as Mad-Eye Moody), *Harry Potter and the Goblet of Fire*

The most terrible curse, the Killing Curse (*Avada Kedavra*), brings death upon its victim with a bright green light. It's the very curse that Voldemort employed when killing Harry's parents.

"*Avada Kedavra* is the particularly nasty one," Emma Watson (Hermione Granger) said, recalling the scene where Mad-Eye shows it to his fourth-year students. "It just kills them straight out, which obviously affected Harry." Watson admitted that she thinks Hermione had a "maternal instinct" to protect her friends in the scene where Mad-Eye demonstrates it to them.

Avada Kedavra was the choice spell of the Dark Lord. He leveled the spell at Harry multiple times, and Harry fended him off all but once—when he chose to sacrifice himself during the Battle of Hogwarts.

Voldemort casts this spell at Harry a final time in the Battle of Hogwarts. Of course, Harry won, with two very special spells.

The Dark Mark

VOLDEMORT AND HARRY'S DUEL

In *Harry Potter and the Deathly Hallows – Part 2*, Harry and Voldemort battle for the final time. Harry and Voldemort's duel spanned two parts. In the first, Harry sacrificed himself in the Forbidden Forest. Voldemort destroyed the Horcrux he inadvertently created when he first cast the Killing Curse at one-year-old Harry. After a conversation with Dumbledore inside his head, Harry then went back to Hogwarts to help find and destroy the last Horcrux—Nagini—which Neville valiantly did.

After the last Horcrux was destroyed, Voldemort could be killed. Harry dueled Voldemort a final time and prevailed.

USED BY VOLDEMORT:
Avada Kedavra

USED BY HARRY:
Confringo
Expelliarmus

USE YOUR WAND
TO REVEAL THE SCENE IN
THE BATTLE OF HOGWARTS.

LOVE

"DO NOT PITY THE DEAD, HARRY. PITY THE LIVING. AND ABOVE ALL, ALL THOSE WHO LIVE WITHOUT LOVE."

—Albus Dumbledore, *Harry Potter and the Deathly Hallows – Part 2*

The Harry Potter films are chock full of enchanting, beautiful, and eye-catching magic, but it was love that makes the story arc complete. Harry's love for his friends and Hogwarts helped turn the tides and wwhelped them win the Wizarding War.

Think about someone you love. Perhaps it's a family member, a friend, a teacher, a guardian, or a Bichon Frise. Using the invisible ink marker within the wand, draw who you love in the next pages. When you're done, the light on the wand can illuminate what you've drawn.